Farmer Christmas

For Hamish, Digby, Noah and Bella

The inspiration for Farmer Christmas, was and always will be,

our wonderful children.

First printed in 2017 by Ashley House Printing Company
Published by Catherine Baddeley and Sophie Baugh-Jones

ISBN 978-1-5272-0744-8

For more information on the book and on future Farmer Christmas titles please go to www.farmerchristmas.net

Text © Catherine Baddeley
Illustrations © Sophie Baugh-Jones

Can you find Rusty the Robin on every page?

Psst... keep reading for the Christmas Eve poem at the back!

Three little children ask their mummy one day, "What does Father Christmas look like and have you seen his sleigh?"
She laughs, "Oh yes, I've seen it and Father Christmas too, I saw him when I was a little girl, about the same age as you!"

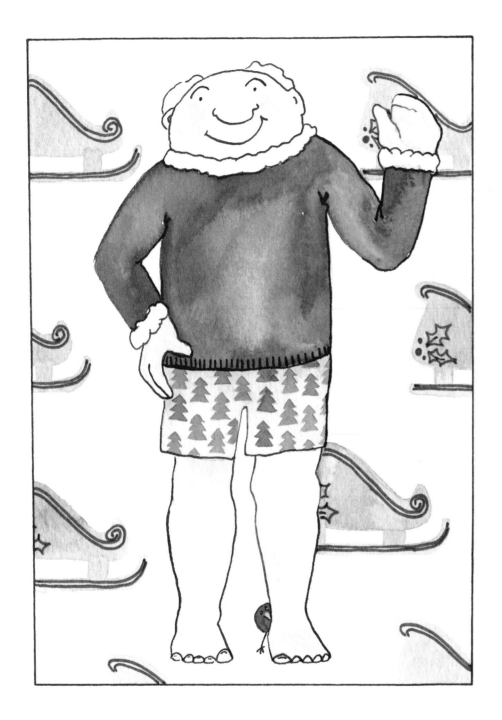 

"He wears a big woolly jumper, which is red with a white fur trim, and his sleigh is packed with presents, right up to the brim. He wears a pair of wellies, which keep his toes all warm, and they're lined with fur and snug inside to keep him dry in a storm."

"What else, what else?" the children cry. "Tell us what you know!"

"Well, he has a big round belly, that wobbles to and fro, and his beard is long and fluffy, all soft and white as snow."

"Is he very jolly mummy and does he always know, whether we've been bad or good and what presents we'd like if so?"

"Oh yes," she laughs, "he's very merry and very clever too, he remembers all the presents... even one for you!"

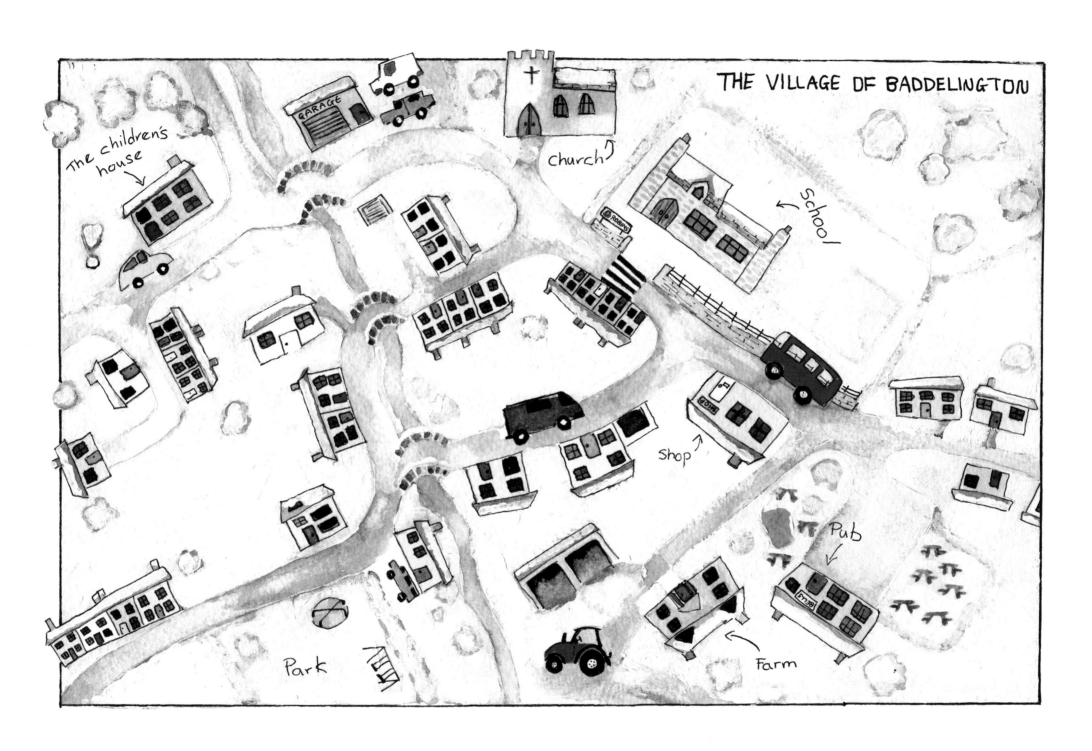

"But where does he live", the children ask, "at other times of year?"

"Why don't you try to find him?" she says. "He may even live quite near!"

"Let's find Father Christmas!" the children shout. "We can ask him about his sleigh...

let's go to the village and see if he's there today!" So off they went to the village, to hunt for a fluffy white beard,

a big fat man with a jolly round face – "We'll find him today," they cheered!

They went to the shop in the village and down the aisles they peered,
but they couldn't see a jolly old man, not even one with a beard.

They went to the park and played all day, but they didn't see a woolly jumper or anything that looked like a sleigh.

But then they see a friendly face, and goodness! What do you know? It's Farmer Nick, who lives nearby,
with a beard as white as snow! He is wearing a red woolly jumper, with fur to keep him warm,
and his wellies are big and snug inside, to keep him dry in a storm.

His face is round and jolly and he does look rather fat, "Are you Father Christmas?" they ask, and he smiles,

giving his tummy a pat. "HO! HO! HO! I'm FARMER CHRISTMAS!" he laughs, his face all jolly and pink,

"I don't have reindeer or a sleigh, but I do have a tractor," he winks.

"Here's my tractor," he points, "it's big and shiny and red."

"But where do all the presents go?" the children excitedly said.

"Well the tractor has a trailer", he says, "which I can easily tow, so the presents go in the trailer and they come wherever I go."

"But how will we see you on Christmas Eve?" the children jump and cry.

"Why, just look out of your window," he laughs, "high up into the sky,

and from your bed you can wave to me, as my tractor flies right by!"

On Christmas Eve...

High on a hill in a big brown shed,
Farmer Christmas is getting out of bed.

He brushes his beard and puts on his hat,
puts on his wellies, gives his tummy a pat.

"Well well well," he says, "it's Christmas Eve,
time to visit all the children that believe.

"With presents and magic and Christmas cheer,
I'll deliver to those who've been good all year"

And how does he deliver all the presents this day?
With his tractor and trailer, used as a sleigh.